Philippe Dupasquier
Jack at Sea

Prentice-Hall Books For Young Readers
A Division of Simon & Schuster, Inc.
New York

Copyright © 1986 by Philippe Dupasquier

Published by Prentice-Hall Books For Young Readers
A Division of Simon & Schuster, Inc.
Simon & Schuster Building
1230 Avenue of the Americas
New York, New York 10020

PRENTICE-HALL BOOKS FOR YOUNG READERS
is a trademark of Simon & Schuster, Inc.
Published in Great Britain by Andersen Press Ltd.

Designed by Philippe Dupasquier

Printed by Grafiche AZ in Italy

10 9 8 7 6 5 4 3 2 1
Library of Congress Cataloguing in Publication Data

Dupasquier, Philippe.
   Jack at Sea.

   Summary: Life aboard a British warship brings Jack
into contact with a naval battle, press gangs, floggings,
and shipwreck, until he finally makes his way home to
England.
   [1. Naval battles—Fiction.   2. Shipwrecks—Fiction.
3. Adventure and adventurers—Fiction.   4. Sea stories]
I. Title
PZ7.D924Jac 1986b   [E]   86-16889
ISBN 0-13-509209-4

McCloud and I had been fishing when we saw the ships.
"Warships!" growled McCloud. "We'll have to watch out in The Three Bells tonight!"

That night the inn was crowded with sailors. McCloud sat quietly in a corner. Then the press-gang burst in. They overpowered McCloud and carted him off to one of their ships.

When all was quiet I swam out to the ship. But by the time I'd climbed aboard I was so tired I crept behind some barrels and went to sleep.

In the morning the crew discovered me. They set me to work in the gunroom below deck. There I found McCloud.

Life was harder on that ship than any I've ever known. The food was rotten, the work was endless and the conditions cramped and cruel.

Once I knocked over a sailor's rum ration. McCloud stood up for me and a fight broke out. McCloud and the sailor were punished. All I could think about that day was mutiny.

But the next day the enemy was sighted. Decks were cleared and battle began. There was no time for anything else.

I had to supply the cannon with gunpowder. On one of my trips to the gunroom I found McCloud on the floor.

"We've been hit, Jack! Get away from here!" he yelled.

I ran back on deck. McCloud was right. The ship was sinking. I jumped clear and grabbed hold of a piece of the wreckage. All night I clung on calling McCloud.

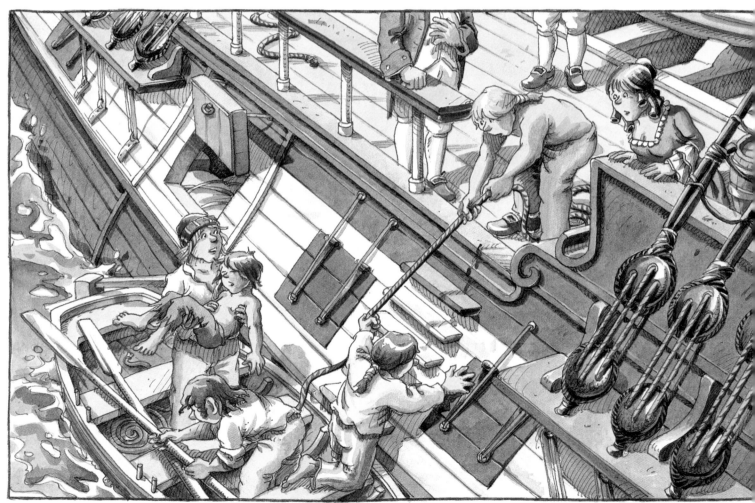

By morning I had given up hope of being rescued. Then I saw a ship on the horizon. It was a merchant ship. The Captain and crew were very kind. So was Mrs Williams, one of the passengers.

She was like a mother to me.

One night I started to cry at the Captain's table. Mrs Williams put me to bed in her cabin and I told her about McCloud.

"I meant to help him," I said.

"And you did," said Mrs Williams. "You were friends at sea. No one could have done more. McCloud is probably sitting in The Three Bells this minute telling them all about it."

Knowing McCloud, Mrs Williams is probably right.

Well, maybe. . .